TILLY'S PONY TAILS

Free Spirit
the mustang

WITHDRAWN

Pippa Funnell began riding when she was very young –
on a pony lent to her by a friend of her mother's.

An Olympic champion, she became the first and (so far)
only person to win eventing's greatest prize, the Rolex
Grand Slam in 2003, riding Primmore's Pride.
She has had countless other successes in her career,
most recently winning the Bramham International Horse
Trials on Redesigned in June 2010. She's also delighted
to have been a member of the British team at the 2010
World Equestrian Games held in Kentucky.
Pippa is proud to be a trustee of World Horse Welfare.
Visit their website at www.worldhorsewelfare.org.

Tilly's Pony Tails mark her brilliant debut in
children's fiction. She lives in Surrey with her husband,
William Funnell, a top class show jumper.

TILLY'S PONY TAILS

Free Spirit
the mustang

PIPPA FUNNELL

Illustrated by Jennifer Miles

Orion
Children's Books

First published in Great Britain in 2012
by Orion Children's Books
a division of the Orion Publishing Group Ltd
Orion House
5 Upper St Martin's Lane
London WC2H 9EA
An Hachette UK Company

1 3 5 7 9 8 6 4 2

A catalogue record for this book is available from the British Library.

ISBN 978 1 4440 0264 5

Printed and bound by CPI Group (UK) Ltd, Coydon, CR0 4YY

www.orionbooks.co.uk
www.tillysponytails.co.uk

For all of you who have read and enjoyed
the Tilly series

The character of Anna in this story takes her name from
a real-life Anna, who is a member of The Pony Club.
Anna won a competition run through The Pony Club
to become a character in a Tilly's Pony Tails book.

To find out more about The Pony Club,
go to www.pcuk.org.

One

'That's it, Magic! Good boy!'

Tilly Redbrow rose in the saddle as her horse, Magic Spirit, performed a rather smart extended trot. She wanted this movement to be perfect. Top marks. No errors. She pictured the faces of the judges, the scoreboards, and the crowds. She imagined herself wearing an elegant dressage top hat and tailcoat and long, polished riding boots.

'And now into halt,' came a distant voice. 'Halt, please!'

Tilly pulled Magic to a muddled stop.
She took the reins in one hand and saluted.

'Didn't you hear me asking you to
halt?' said Angela, her instructor.

'Yes. Er, I mean, no. I was, um, I guess
I was a bit lost in the moment,' Tilly said,
blushing.

'I could see that,' said Angela. 'Where
were you this time? At the Olympics? Or
Badminton?'

'The Rolex Kentucky Three Day Event,' said Tilly. 'The top event in America.'

'Of course,' said Angela. 'I should have known. I guess Silver Shoe Farm can't compete with the excitement of a real four star event. Not long now. You and Brook must be so excited.

I'm sorry for being so agitated. I guess I'm starting to get more nervous too now that it's a matter of days rather than weeks before we leave.'

Tilly understood why Angela had been getting gradually more twitchy over the past few months. As the day of their departure approached, Angela had been putting endless hours of work into preparing her beloved event horse, Pride and Joy, for the Rolex Kentucky Three Day Event. Ever since Tilly and the girls at Silver Shoe had begged Angela to bring Pride and Joy out of retirement and give him another chance at competing, their partnership had never looked back. Having had so many years off, it was quite remarkable that there had been no sign of Pride's old injury, and just as remarkable that Angela had been able to step back into the highest level of the sport.

Tilly was as excited as Angela was nervous. To her delight, Angela had asked Tilly to be her groom for the week, and Tilly's brother, Brook, was also joining them on the trip. He had persuaded his parents to let him go for the experience of seeing top riders at their very best.

'I never realised how much extra work had to be done to get horses fit enough for a three day,' said Tilly. 'I hope it all works out.'

'So do I,' said Angela cautiously. 'It's a big challenge after so many years, and we'll

be up against some of the best riders in the world. It takes a very special horse to do well at a three day event. In the dressage, they have to be responsive, supple and elegant, and with so many more people watching, it creates an electric atmosphere.'

'It must be very distracting for horses and riders,' said Tilly.

'Yes, it really tests the concentration. That's why in all the training, we work to teach our horses to respond to us, despite distractions. For the cross-country, horses need to be brave, athletic and very fit. And for the show jumping on the final day they need to be able to jump a clear round.'

It sounded thrilling, but extremely tough. Tilly had already been to Badminton and she'd seen clips of Kentucky on the internet, so she knew it was going to be demanding. The cross-country course covered four miles, with thirty jumps, and the show jumping required horses to clear a height of 1.3 metres.

'Wow. I can see why you've been working so hard over the past few months,' said Tilly.

'Yes, but remember it's a team effort, and grooming is an invaluable role. I know I can trust you to look after Pride and Joy.'

Tilly grinned. The idea of grooming at such a major event made her feel nervous, as well as excited, so she appreciated Angela's words of encouragement.

After her dressage lesson, Tilly led Magic back to the yard and tied him up.

'Let me get you a drink,' she said. 'You must be thirsty after that. Who knows? Maybe one day it'll be you and me competing at Kentucky. I suppose we'd better work on our halt though. We were a bit messy today!'

Magic shook his head. Tilly gave him a pat then carried his bucket to the water tap and filled it. As she reached down she noticed one of her horsehair bracelets had come loose. Some of the hairs had frayed and didn't look as if they'd last much longer.

'Oh, no! I must have caught it on something!'

The bracelets were very important to Tilly. They were made from the tail-hairs of the special horses in her life. She made them for her friends, and wore three of her own.

One was from Magic's tail. Another was from the tail-hairs of Stripy, a zebra foal she'd helped rescue while on a safari holiday with Brook. And the other, the one that was coming loose, she'd had since she was born. She and Brook had each been given a bracelet by their birth mum, before she died.

Tilly and Brook believed their bracelets were Native American and that, years ago, their mum had spent some time living with a tribe. They'd been in contact with a man called Chief Four Paws, whose people watched over free-roaming wild Mustangs.

Tilly inspected the damage. The bracelet was secure but she hated the thought that it might fall off without her noticing.

'I can't lose it, Magic,' she said. 'It's one of the only links I have to my past. But how on earth am I going to repair it? I don't think there are many wild Mustangs roaming the streets of North Cosford!'

Just then, her phone rang. It was Brook.

'Hi,' she said. 'How are you?'

'Busy,' he replied. 'I've been trying to sort out a programme for Solo while we're away. I've managed to persuade a friend to keep riding him for me.' Tilly knew that Brook had a few ambitions of his own with Solo – he was hoping to get selected later in the season for the Junior British team. 'I can't believe we're really going to the USA! Are you looking forward to it?'

'Are you kidding?' said Tilly. 'I can't wait!'

Two

It had taken lots of persuasion, but when Tilly's parents had finally agreed to her going to Kentucky, they'd had some conditions. First, she needed to catch up on all the school work she was going to miss. Luckily, Tilly's school had agreed to this too. Second, she had to wash the car and do the vacuuming for a month, in order to contribute to the cost of the flight. She didn't mind the extra work involved. It would be worth it. And, secretly, she knew her parents were pleased for her.

'We know how much this means to you, Tiger Lil',' said her dad, as they sat at the dinner table that evening. 'Maybe one day you'll be grooming full-time for top riders and doing it professionally?'

'Maybe,' said Tilly. 'But as much as I enjoy grooming, Dad, I think I'd rather be one of the top riders!'

'That's my girl!'

Whatever Tilly's dreams for the future were, she knew that grooming at a major international competition was a good place to start. It was a chance to see some of the most experienced riders and horses in action, and hopefully learn a few tricks from their grooms.

After dinner, she went into the lounge and switched on the downstairs computer. Scruff, the family's long-haired Jack Russell, watched from his basket. She found a chat forum where professional grooms talked about their daily routines, which included mucking out, feeding, exercising the horses, clipping and trimming them, sweeping yards, cleaning tack, grooming and tacking up. At shows and competitions, the role also involved loading equipment, plaiting up, holding the horse in the ring, checking on the horse at night, and some grooms even drove the horsebox.

Suddenly, Tilly felt a nervous flutter in her stomach. None of these duties would be new to her, but it was such an important competition for Angela, and she wanted to

do it all perfectly. At least she would have Brook to help her.

Just then an email came through from Angela.

Hey, Tilly.
Pride and Joy has just been picked up by a transporter, along with the four other British horses that are going to Kentucky. They are on the way to the airport – Liz, the team vet, will be travelling with them. I hope he's okay, I wish he didn't have to fly four days before us.
See you tomorrow anyway.
Angela x

Ahead of his flight, Angela had to sort out the documents for Pride and Joy – including passport, vaccinations and vets' certificates proving that he was disease-free prior to entering the United States.

Tilly knew it would be hard for Angela to be separated from Pride and Joy – it wasn't only the flight, but the quarantine period too. She hated being apart from Magic for more than a day. But it was exciting to think that very soon they would be arriving at the Kentucky Horse Park and getting ready for the competition. She smiled to herself. She was just about to send a reassuring reply when she saw she had another email from Brook.

Hi T,

Guess what? I emailed Chief Four Paws ages ago to tell him that we were going to Kentucky. I've just had a reply and he says he's going to be there too. He'll be staying at the Kentucky Horse Park. Not only that, he's got his special horse, Free Spirit, competing in the Reining Championships. I looked it up and apparently they're a sort of Western riding competition where riders guide their horses through a precise pattern of circles, spins and stops, all done in a slow canter called a lope. They're on at the Horse Park at the same time as the Rolex. So excited!

B. x

Tilly sat back and took a deep breath. She couldn't believe how lucky she was. Meeting Chief Four Paws would turn a brilliant trip into an amazing one.

When the day before the trip finally came, Tilly spent her last few hours at Silver Shoe, grooming, feeding and mucking out Magic's stable. Once she'd finished in the yard, she took him down to the field to graze.

'I won't be gone long,' she told him, stroking his neck. 'Just a week. But, somehow, I think it's going to be one of the best weeks of my life!'

Magic swished his tail and let out a snort.

'Of course, it would be even better if you were coming with me.'

'Come on, Tiger Lil',' said a voice behind her.

It was her dad. He'd come to pick her up. They were having a family meal that evening, then an early night. Tilly's dad had volunteered to take the three of them to the airport next morning.

'Your mum says dinner's nearly ready,' he said. 'We need to get going.'

'Coming,' she said, sighing. 'Goodbye, Magic! Love you.'

She tickled Magic's ear, fed him a carrot then kissed his cheek and walked away.

They arrived at the airport bright and early. When Tilly had said goodbye to her dad, she, Angela and Brook made their way excitedly to the check-in desk. Then, after looking around the airport shops for a while and picking up last minute extras, it was time to board their flight.

To Tilly, it didn't seem so very long ago that she and Brook had been on a plane on their way back from their horse safari in Botswana, where Tilly had helped a stranded zebra foal.

'Are you feeling okay?' Tilly asked Angela, as they tucked into their complimentary snacks. Angela had been quiet all morning.

'I can't stop worrying about Pride. I just wish I could have travelled with him.'

Angela had had a phone call from the team vet, Liz, the night before, telling her that Pride and the other horses had flown well and landed safely. They were at an airport a couple of hours away from the Kentucky Horse Park, waiting to be transported to the quarantine station. But she hadn't heard anything since, and Tilly could sense she was growing more and more uneasy.

'How long do they have to stay in quarantine for?' asked Brook.

'Three days, it's compulsory for any horse entering the USA.'

'The only good thing is that Liz, and a lovely woman called Polly, who works for the international horse transport company will be staying with them,' said Angela.

Tilly knew Angela had immediately warmed to Polly when she'd arrived to

collect Pride. Polly had flown with horses
for many years. 'They travel better on a
plane than they do on a lorry,' she'd told
Angela. 'I'll keep a close eye on him the
whole way, he'll have plenty of hay and
water, and he'll be fine. Don't worry about
a thing.'

Angela was worrying anyway, but there
wasn't anything they could do except
wait now. Tilly squeezed Angela's arm in
what she hoped was a reassuring way, and
crossed her fingers. Then, while Angela
busied herself with a Sudoku puzzle,
she and Brook settled down to watch the
in-flight films.

Three

When they landed at Cincinnati International Airport, they were all exhausted after the eight and a half hour flight. It was only around lunchtime, but it felt much later. Still, all three of them, and especially Angela, were desperate to see Pride.

As they came through the arrivals gate, they were met by a tall man wearing a cowboy hat. He was holding a notice with 'Kentucky Horse Park' written on it.

'I guess that must be our driver,' said Angela, as they made their way towards him.

'Howdy, I'm Gus,' said the man, in a strong southern American drawl. 'At your service. I'll be driving you to the great event.'

'I'm Angela Fisher,' said Angela, shaking his hand.

Brook introduced himself, then put his arm around Tilly.

'This is my sister, Tilly Redbrow. She's going to be grooming for Angela. I'm along for the ride – as chief supporter and general dogsbody!'

'My water bucket carrier,' said Tilly, laughing.

'You must be keen to get to the event and catch up with your horse,' said Gus. 'I saw the transporters bringing the horses from the quarantine station early this morning. I should think they've settled in by now.'

'Wow, I can see why Kentucky is known as the blue grass state,' said Angela,

admiring the long lush grass covering the
rolling hills, as they sped along the wide
freeway.

Tilly knew they must be getting close
to the Horse Park when they began to
drive past field after field full of beautiful
thoroughbreds, some with mares and foals.
The fields were all immaculate with
white post and rail fencing. She asked
Gus about it.

'Oh sure, many of the top racehorses in America are bred at these stud farms here in Kentucky,' he explained.

When they finally arrived at the Horse Park, Gus dropped Angela, Tilly and Brook at the passes office where they could collect all their documents and were pointed in the direction of the stables.

There were horses everywhere, looking over their stable doors, all interested in exploring their new surroundings. Tilly could see block after block, open fronted with sliding doors, with a large overhang where you could tie your horse up outside but still be under cover.

'There's Polly,' said Angela, quickening her step. 'She's coming out of that last stable over there.'

'How's my boy?' asked Angela, hurrying past Polly towards the open stable door.

Tilly noticed Polly had a concerned look on her face.

'Is everything okay?' she asked. She followed Angela into the stable.

Inside, Liz, the vet, was running her hand down one of Pride's front legs.

'Please don't tell me it's his old injury,' said Angela, her voice slightly panicky.

'I'm sure it's nothing like that,' replied Liz. 'He must have knocked it on his way here from the quarantine station, that's all. It looks sore but I'm confident it's not a serious problem.'

'He flew so well and he has been so good in quarantine,' said Polly. 'Honestly, he's been fine. Oh, but I can't help feeling responsible.'

'Horses will be horses. I know you did everything possible to ensure they had a safe journey,' Angela said, trying to make Polly feel better. She gave Pride a hug. He was obviously delighted to see her.

Angela turned to Tilly.

'It looks as though you'll have to

work some of your magic on Pride, as you did with Red Admiral all that time ago.' To Polly and Liz, she explained, 'Red Admiral's a racehorse who came back from injury and won a big race, thanks to Tilly's love and attention. This girl's special, I'm very lucky to have her grooming for me.'

'Why don't I start my duties now and take him over to hose his leg for twenty minutes?' said Tilly.

'Good idea,' said Liz.

'Brook, could you help me lift this trunk, please?'

Brook and Angela lifted the heavy trunk, which contained all of Angela and Pride's equipment for the competition. They put it in an empty stable opposite Pride's. This was to be their tack room for the week.

Meanwhile, Tilly led Pride and Joy to the hose.

'Well done for coping with the flight,' said Tilly. 'And don't worry about your poor leg. We'll have you sorted in no time.'

Pride gave a friendly whinny and rubbed his nose against her shoulder. She patted his neck and began thinking about her duties as a groom – how neatly she could plait his mane and how glossy she could get his coat. She wanted him to look his very best for every day of the competition. But most of all, she wanted his leg to be okay. She smiled encouragingly, held her horsehair bracelets and made a wish that everything would be all right.

Four

'This place is enormous!' said Brook, as he, Tilly and Angela walked to the campground.

'There are over a hundred horses stabled here permanently,' said Angela. 'But when competitions take place, hundreds of additional horses, like Pride, are flown in from all over the world. '

Everywhere they looked there were horses of different breeds and colours. Some were being petted in the barns.

Some were being ridden in the paddocks. Some were quietly grazing.

'It's a horse city!' said Tilly. 'I love it! It's Badminton, but on a much bigger scale!'

She thought how much she'd like to bring Magic. It seemed to be a place where horses took priority over people, where they were honoured and cherished. She knew she was going to enjoy her time here.

Tilly and Brook unpacked their things then relaxed for a while. They were exhausted from the long flight, so after an early dinner, they were all very happy to fall into their beds.

As she lay awake that night, Tilly thought about Magic Spirit again. She wondered what he was up to and looked forward to telling him about the Horse Park and Pride's first flight. She decided to send a text to Mia:

HEY. HOW R U? KENTUCKY = COOL! HOPE SS IS OKAY.
BIG HUGS TO MAGIC. XX

Mia replied straightaway:

SS BUSY AS ALWAYS. DUNCAN SAYS HI. MAGIC SAYS SNORT-
NEIGH-SNORT...WHICH TRANSLATES AS I LOVE TILLY!
WISH ANGELA LUCK FOR US. LOTS OF LOVE, M XX

Tilly smiled. Over the next two days Angela would be able to spend time familiarising herself with the cross-country course and the main arena, and then it would begin – with the dressage test. She glanced over at Brook. Although he was pretending to read a magazine, she could tell he was thinking about it too.

Next morning, Tilly dressed in a navy polo-shirt, her favourite powder-blue jodhpurs and a pair of tan riding boots. She, Angela and Brook went to check on Pride. When they got to the stables, the stable manager, whose name was Esme, was there to greet them.

'By the way,' Esme said. 'There's a man looking for you, calls himself Chief Four Paws. He told me to let you guys know he's here.'

Tilly and Brook looked at each other. Tilly's stomach filled with butterflies.

'Where is he now?' said Brook.

'Oh, he's out riding. He's brought the most beautiful horse with him, a Mustang, named Free Spirit. Told me the horse is old, but still moves like a four year old! He's competing in the Free Reining Championships this year. You've got to see him!'

Free Spirit. Tilly loved the name. Of course. It was so like Magic Spirit.

Angela looked at her watch.

'Maybe you guys can catch up with him later. Let's see if we can track down Liz to check Pride's leg. I'm sure it will be fine, but it would be good to have that extra reassurance.'

'I'll stay with Pride,' said Tilly. 'I suppose my grooming duties officially start today.'

'Thanks,' said Angela. 'In that case, I'm going to look for Liz and then I might take a walk around the cross-country course, figure out some of the jumps. Brook, do you want to join me? I'd appreciate a second opinion.'

'Sure,' said Brook. 'Let's go.'

'Hello, boy,' Tilly whispered, as she peered over Pride's door. 'Or should I say, howdy?'

Pride pricked his ears. He finished the mouthful of hay he was munching and turned towards her. Tilly opened the door and stepped inside.

'This is nice,' she said. 'Very cosy.'

Pride lowered his head and scratched his neck against a wooden beam.

'Got an itch?' said Tilly.

She rubbed his neck, then ran her hand

across his shoulder, and down to his foreleg. Immediately, she noticed it was warm.

'Uh oh,' she whispered, crouching down to take a closer look. 'That's not good.'

She massaged the leg and felt a gentle heat radiating from it. She remembered how Brian, the vet from Silver Shoe, had explained that heat in a limb could be a sign of injury. The problem with the leg had obviously got worse.

Pride didn't appear to be in any discomfort as he stood or walked, but fast paces were a different matter.

'Don't worry, boy,' she said. 'Hopefully, it's nothing, but we'll have to be careful. We've got to protect those legs of yours.'

She was dreading breaking the news to Angela, but she knew that Angela wouldn't want to take any chances with Pride's health. She told Esme, the stable manager, about the problem and as Liz wasn't about yet, Esme agreed to get one of the Park

vets to look at it.

'Nothing too sinister,' said the vet calmly, after her inspection. 'Just a bit of tenderness, from where he knocked it.'

Tilly sighed with relief.

'My advice is to get the ice-cold hose on it as often as possible. I'll check on it again tomorrow.'

'Thanks,' said Tilly.

Now she felt a lot happier about telling Angela. She stroked Pride's nose, then went out to the yard. As she filled Pride's water bucket, Tilly looked up and saw a horse and rider. They were silhouetted in the sunlight against the bright blue sky. The horse was small and sturdy, with a short neck crest. The rider had long, dark flowing hair and was wearing a suede fringed jacket. Tilly guessed straightaway who it was.

'Chief Four Paws!'

She ran towards them, unable to contain her excitement. He looked down at her. She gazed back, in awe.

'You must be Tilly!' he said. His voice
was deep and serene, just as Tilly had
imagined it would be.

He jumped from the horse.

'We meet at last. How was your
journey?'

'Long,' said Tilly, with a slight squeak in her voice. She couldn't take her eyes off the Chief, or his horse. It was hard to believe they were really standing in front of her.

'And your brother, Brook? And Angela? And Pride? How are they?'

'Brook's good,' said Tilly. 'He'll be so pleased to finally meet you. Pride's fine too. He travelled well, but, oh . . .'

Her smile faded.

'What's wrong?'

'It's his leg,' she explained. 'There's bit of heat in his front left shin. The vet thinks it will be okay. But I'm keeping my fingers crossed.'

'Fingers crossed isn't enough for such a major competition,' said Chief Four Paws, frowning. 'Do you mind if I take a look?'

The Chief handed Tilly the reins of his horse.

'This is Free Spirit,' he said. 'One of the finest Mustangs in our herd. He comes

44

everywhere with me and this year he's competing in the Reining Championships.'

Tilly took the reins and ran her hand across Free Spirit's shoulder.

His coat was a black silver dapple, with light patches and a sooty mane and tail. He was compact, only 15 hh or so. She patted his neck, and as she looked into his face, she noticed his eyes were a striking pale blue colour. She'd never seen blue eyes on a horse before. They were mesmerising.

'Wow, his eyes are amazing,' she said.

'Yes, he inherited them from his father. Some people think blue eyes on a horse are a sign of sight problems, but it's not necessarily the case. Free Spirit can see as well as any horse.'

Free Spirit rubbed his nose against Tilly's palm and sniffed her horsehair bracelets. He was very keen and inquisitive. With his silvery coat, he reminded her a little of Magic Spirit, but mostly he reminded her of the horse in the only photograph that Tilly had of her mum. That horse had been a wild Mustang too. She felt a connection to Free Spirit instantly.

And from the way he studied her with his strange, pale eyes, she wondered if he felt it too.

Five

As Chief Four Paws was about to enter
Pride's stable, Angela and Brook appeared.
They hadn't been able to find Liz
anywhere and Angela was looking a little
flustered. Brook recognised the Chief
instantly.

'I'm honoured to meet you,' he said, as
they greeted each other.

'The honour is mine,' said Chief Four
Paws, then he shook Angela's hand. 'Pride
looks like a very fine horse.'

'He is,' Angela agreed. 'Which is just as well. We've just seen some seriously big jumps on the cross-country course. The water ditch is a monster! I really hope his leg is okay. Did Tilly tell you?'

The Chief nodded.

'One of the Park vets has had a look,' Tilly said. 'She's optimistic.'

Tilly explained the treatment. Angela listened carefully.

'Sounds like good advice,' said the Chief. 'Do you mind if I take a look too?'

'Of course,' said Angela. She caught Tilly's eye and smiled.

Chief Four Paws went into the stable and began massaging Pride's leg. Brook, Angela and Tilly stood at the door with Free Spirit and watched. Tilly saw that the Chief was wearing at least ten different horsehair bracelets around his wrist. He'd obviously worked with many wonderful horses.

'I agree with the vet,' he said. 'It doesn't seem to be anything more than a minor inflammation.'

'What about the competition?' said Angela anxiously. 'Do you think he'll be okay?'

Chief Four Paws stood up and rubbed his chin.

'As the vet suggested, hose the leg down with cold water for twenty minutes, as many times a day as possible. I expect if we can draw the heat out and reduce the swelling, the leg will be perfect. I've spent my whole life taking care of horses. I see this sort of thing all the time.

Something I've noticed is that recovery
is often quicker if injured horses aren't
isolated. After all, their instinct is to be part
of a herd. We should let Pride and Free
Spirit stable next to each other.'

'Sounds good,' said Tilly, impressed by
Chief Four Paw's wisdom.

They wasted no time. Angela and the
Chief discussed competition strategies,
while Tilly and Brook gave Pride's leg
another hose down. Brook ran the cold,
icy water and Tilly massaged it to improve
blood circulation to the muscles and
tendons. She remembered watching
Jack Fisher do the same for Red Admiral
when he'd injured his leg.

Pride didn't mind. In fact, he seemed
to be enjoying all the attention. After
twenty minutes they stopped the treatment
and led Pride into the yard, so he could get

to know Free Spirit.

Tilly, Brook, Angela and Chief Four
Paws watched as the two horses stood
together, swishing flies with their tails.
Occasionally, one would look up at the
other, prick his ears and make a wickering
noise.

'They seem happy,' said Tilly.

'Yes,' said Chief Four Paws. 'I knew Free Spirit would have a positive effect on Pride. He's a mature, experienced horse. He's a protector of other horses and has a generous heart.'

Tilly could see pride and love in the Chief's eyes.

'Have you had Free Spirit a long time?' she asked.

'He'll be ten years old next month,' said the Chief. 'I was there at his birth, helping Running River, who was Chief before me. We have many fantastic horses in our herd, but Free Spirit is very special. His father was an amazing, mysterious horse, a fine stallion, also called Free Spirit. The original, you might say. He was leader of one of the largest Mustang herds in America. Our tribe had an agreement with the local town whereby we supplied twenty horses a year, as a gesture of good will and peace between our communities. But Free Spirit was so wild, and extremely protective of his herd, it became increasingly difficult to fulfil our promise.'

Tilly nodded, fascinated by the story.

'What happened?'

'Running River was a wonderful horseman. Horses trusted him; they felt a sort of connection with him. It took time, but Running River built a strong bond with Free Spirit. He made a breakthrough where no other man had succeeded, and managed to calm his wild nature. And so this beautiful stallion became less aggressive, and we were able to supply the horses as we'd promised, and continue watching over the free-roaming Mustangs as we always have done. Free Spirit is legendary among our people.'

'Amazing!' said Brook, putting his arm around Tilly.

'One of the reasons I wanted you both to meet him,' said the Chief, 'is because I think he will be special to you too. When Running River saw the photograph you sent, you already know that he recognised your mother, Sweet Rose. Like him, she

also had the ability to understand horses. And the horse in your photograph is that famous wild stallion I told you of, the very first Free Spirit. This horse, his son, is like a living connection between the past and the present.'

Tilly thought about the only photograph she had of her birth mum – standing with a beautiful Mustang. She thought of all the times she'd wondered about that horse, and about her mum. And now she had another part of the puzzle. She reached up and stroked the young Free Spirit's shoulder, running her fingers over his warm, glossy coat. She imagined her mum doing the same, her hands in the same place as Tilly's were now. It felt amazing.

Free Spirit lowered his head and stared at her.

'Wow,' she whispered, her heart beating fast.

Six

In the days before the competition began, the heat and tenderness in Pride's leg eased off. Angela took Pride out for a few pipe openers and short gallops and practised some jumps, and she and Tilly were both impressed at the recovery he'd made. They were even more delighted when the vet gave Pride the all-clear to compete.

They continued to give him the cold water therapy, just to be certain. They did it morning, noon and evening. Tilly also made sure Pride had his vitamins and supplements and that his general health was good. After all, he was about to take part in the hardest competition of his life.

He and Free Spirit continued to stable side-by-side, often bobbing their heads over the doors to admire one another. Standing in the yard, when Free Spirit flicked his mane, so did Pride. When Free Spirit looked for shade, so did Pride. And when Free Spirit decided to snort as he was being groomed, so did Pride.

It was lovely to see the horses responding to one another. Tilly could see what Chief Four Paws meant about Free Spirit. He was obviously a horse who nurtured others, because even though Pride was a large, headstrong Thoroughbred, he seemed to trust the little Mustang.

That evening, Tilly gave Pride a thorough wash and brush so that he'd look his best for the dressage test. She also checked all his tack and equipment and made sure everything was ready for the morning.

As she polished his saddle, she noticed her horsehair bracelet – the one that had been damaged – was now hanging by a few threads.

'Oh, no!' she cried, clasping it to her wrist.

She couldn't bear the thought of not wearing it – these bracelets were her good luck charms – but she knew she risked losing it completely if she left it as it was. She sighed.

Then, as she watched Pride nickering to Free Spirit, Tilly suddenly realised she might have the solution. The bracelet had been given to her by her birth mum, and she and Brook had guessed it had been made from the tail-hairs of one of the tribe's Mustangs. So it made perfect sense that it should be repaired with tail-hairs from another Mustang!

Tilly went to Free Spirit's stable.

'Hey, boy!' she said. She reached up to

stroke his nose. 'Do you believe in luck?'

He gazed at her, pale eyes glistening.

'Isn't it strange that just when I need some Mustang tail-hairs, you happen to be around?'

'I call it fate,' said a voice behind her.

She jumped. It was Chief Four Paws.

'Here,' he said, taking her wrist. 'Let me help. I've made thousands of these.'

He inspected the damaged bracelet, then ran his hands through Free Spirit's tail and returned with several coarse, dark hairs.

'They're a good match,' he said.

'They are, aren't they?' said Tilly, intrigued.

Chief Four Paws plaited the new hairs into the bracelet. His fingers worked quickly and they reminded Tilly of her own talent for plaiting. Whether it was a horse's mane before a show, a horsehair bracelet, or even her own hair, which she always wore in plaits, she was often praised for her neatness and skill. As she watched the Chief, she began to wonder. The matching hairs seemed important somehow, but she couldn't quite work out why.

'Tell me about your bracelets,' she said, admiring the Chief's collection.

'I have one from every horse that I've reared or worked with. They're all special to me, but I have some favourites.'

He picked out a pinkish-white one.

'This came from a naughty cremello mare called Little Fire. She used to break through the fences to steal food from the reserve stores. But I liked that about her. She was super smart. She had a look that made you think she knew better than you.'

He held up another. It was dark brown.

'This one came from Returning Moon, a wonderful old chestnut. He died last year, at the age of twenty-three, but he was the biggest horse we've ever had in our herd. And a great watchman.'

'I'd love to meet some of these horses,' said Tilly.

'You and Brook will have to come to the reserve one day,' said the Chief. 'Next

time you're in America. But for now, you can take a little bit of Mustang spirit back to England with you. There. Your bracelet's fixed and should be strong for good.'

'Thanks,' said Tilly. She paused. 'Um, did you ever . . . I mean, Brook and I were wondering . . . did you ever find out anything more about our mum? You said you'd talk to your elders . . .'

'I think you already know the most important thing,' said Chief Four Paws. 'That your mother had a great love and understanding of horses, just like you two.'

Tilly smiled, but suddenly she could see Chief Four Paws was looking serious.

'What is it?'

'I've been waiting to tell you this,' he said. 'I did talk to the tribe elders who remembered her. They said that the thing she most wanted to do was help look after our herd. She was very good with the horses. Running River, our old Chief, remembered her. He said his son, Rapid

Water, was particularly close to her, that
they were in love. They had a baby boy
together.'

'Oh?' said Tilly, eyes wide. 'Do you
think . . . ?'

'. . .that Rapid Water was Brook's and
your father? I think it's highly possible.'

Tilly gasped. She could feel a flutter in
her heart.

'What happened to him?'

'I'm sorry, Tilly. He was killed in a
stampede. Running River told me that
your mother was devastated. He tried to
comfort her. He told her that she could
stay with the tribe, but she found it too
difficult to live with the memories. One
day, she disappeared. He later learned she
had returned to England and that's the last
he knew, until you and Brook got in touch.
Running River is your grandfather.'

Chief Four Paws put his hand on Tilly's
shoulder.

She felt her eyes fill with tears. A long-
lost family. It sounded like something out

of a film, and yet it had really happened. It was her life.

'I know it's a story of sadness,' said the Chief. 'But you must try to take some happiness from it too. You and Brook are wonderful young people and there is no doubt that the remarkable horsemanship of Running River and Rapid Water lives on within you both. In fact, you should consider yourselves part of our tribe. Running River has asked me to tell you that if you ever want to get in contact with him, you'd be welcome.'

Tilly sniffed and smiled. Suddenly, she felt closer to her birth mum than she ever had before. For the first time she'd found out something about her father. And now she'd discovered a grandfather she'd never even known about. The Chief was right. It was a sad story, but it made her feel happy to know about her past, and lucky to have inherited such a wonderful gift.

Seven

Later that day, Tilly and the Chief told Brook what they knew. Like Tilly, the news made him feel sad and happy at the same time, but they were both cheered by the thought of meeting Running River one day, and the thought that their family was so closely linked to the horses they loved so much.

'Maybe we could visit the reserve some day?' said Tilly. 'That would be brilliant.'

In the evening, to take her mind off the competition, Angela had booked tickets for her, Tilly and Brook to see a rodeo show. Chief Four Paws came as their guest,

'I think we're in for a treat,' said Angela. 'I've heard Kentucky cowboys are some of the finest bareback bronco riders around! Isn't that right, Chief?'

'Actually, I think my people are the finest bareback bronco riders around!' he replied, winking at Tilly and Brook. 'No one knows horses like we do!'

When they arrived, they could hear the sound of mooing cattle, loud speakers and country music. There were cars and horse trailers parked in lines in front of a large floodlit outdoor arena. Everyone was dressed in jeans and cowboy boots, and the air was thick with barbecue smoke.

Angela sniffed.

'Mmm. Smells good. I'm starving. I need a pre-competition energy boost.

I can't believe I'll be doing my dressage
test tomorrow! I'm so glad Pride has made
a full recovery.'

'How about some hickory smoked ribs?'
said a stall-owner. 'They're the best!'

Angela and Brook shared a bucket of
ribs and Tilly chose something called a
Super Deluxe Ranch Special, which turned
out to be the biggest beef burger she'd ever
eaten.

They went inside the stadium and Tilly
immediately felt the energy of the place.
The sound of cheering was overwhelming.
She caught Brook's eye and could tell he
was thinking the same as her. Especially
now that they knew horsemanship wasn't
just a hobby any more, it was part of their
heritage.

In the middle of a fenced dirt arena,
a man in a denim shirt was clinging onto a
bucking horse. No saddle, no reins. He was
simply holding on, with all his strength,
to a set of rodeo rigging straps. Tilly stared
in awe.

'That's how to ride!'

Seconds later it was all over. The man
was on the floor. He staggered to his feet
and rubbed his arm.

'Ouch!' said Brook.

'Bronco riding is the toughest of all the
rodeo sports,' said the Chief. 'But these
boys are competing for a rodeo belt-buckle,
so they'll give it everything they've got.
A buckle is one of the most prized trophies

of the rodeo world. Riders need to stay on for at least eight seconds to gain maximum points. Doesn't sound like long, but when you're actually up there . . .'

'I think I'll stick to three-day events,' said Angela.

Next morning, Tilly woke early. She splashed cold water on her face and brushed her teeth. Once she was dressed, she went straight to the stables. It was the first day of the competition. Dressage.

The sun was bright and the air was scented with honeysuckle. The yard was already busy and the atmosphere was electric. Grooms were plaiting and brushing. Riders were pacing up and down nervously.

Tilly greeted Pride, mucked out, refreshed his hay, then prepared for his cold water treatment. As soon as he saw the

hose, he stepped forward. He seemed to understand what was going to happen and waited patiently while Tilly turned the tap on. Once this was done, she combed his mane and began to plait it.

'They're so neat!' said a girl who'd been busily brushing a large chestnut. She looked about Tilly's age, with long, glossy brown hair and rosy cheeks. 'Hi. My name's Anna. I'm grooming for a horse called Bright Star. I wish I could get my plaits as tight as yours. Will you show me?'

'Sure,' said Tilly. She'd noticed Anna with the chestnut the day before, but hadn't had a chance to say hello.

Tilly beckoned Anna over and showed her how she dampened the hair, separated it into sections, plaited it, then secured it with bands.

'You make it look easy,' said Anna. 'Your horse is so beautiful. I hope he does well today. I like your bracelets, by the way. Did you make them yourself?'

70

'I made these two,' said Tilly, pointing
to the bracelets from Magic and Stripy.
'But this one is Native American.'

'Wow!'

Eventually, Angela appeared. She
looked smart in her tailcoat and top hat.
She gave Tilly a tense smile.

'Are you ready?' said Tilly.

'As ready as I'll ever be! We'd better go.'

Tilly checked Pride's tack and rubbed
his coat down. She could feel he was a little
twitchy. Several times, he played with his
bit and shook his mane.

'It's usual for him to be on edge,'

71

said Angela. 'He gets worked up before competing. I think it helps him.'

She mounted and took Pride to warm up.

'How does he feel?' said Tilly, who had followed on behind.

'Great,' Angela replied. 'Really great! I don't think either of us has ever felt this fresh before. Chief Four Paws was right.'

'I knew he would be,' said Tilly.

Together, they led Pride to the dressage arena. Neither of them spoke, although they were both bursting with excitement.

Tilly stood at the side with some of the other grooms. Everyone seemed friendly, but she was glad to chat to Anna, who seemed a lot like her. As they waited, Anna told her all about her horse at home. He was a palomino Irish sport horse, called Flint, and Anna loved spending as much time with him as possible. Tilly told her about Magic too. They talked about Pride and Bright Star and how exciting it was to be at Kentucky. They swapped mobile numbers and promised to meet up when they were back in England.

'Good luck today,' said Anna. 'I hope Pride does well!'

When Angela and Pride walked out in front of the judges Tilly felt enormously proud. There was no sign of discomfort in Pride's leg. In fact, his paces were more graceful and effortless than ever.

Angela looked a little nervous, but she sat up tall and commanded with authority. Pride completed all his movements, including a counter canter, pirouette and flying change, without error. His half-pass was a bit unsteady, but still, the judges gave him good marks.

Tilly's pulse raced. She gripped the fencepost and leaned forward.

'Well done!' she shouted.

Eight

'That was fantastic! You could win!' Tilly said, as they walked Pride back to his stable. 'Really, you could!'

'There's a long way to go yet, Tilly,' said Angela. 'I'm just glad of the opportunity to take part and that Pride's leg seems to be fine.'

She turned and stroked Pride's shoulder.

'Well done! You performed beautifully this morning.'

Pride gave a nicker and shook his head, taking it all in his stride.

Tilly met up with Brook and they spent the rest of the day watching the other competitors. Angela went to get some rest, because the toughest parts of the competition were still to come.

'Early nights, all round,' she said. 'We need to conserve our energy.'

After a good night's sleep, Tilly jumped out of bed and could only think about one thing: cross-country. She loved the finesse of dressage and the skill of show jumping, but nothing compared to the sheer thrill and drama of the cross-country. She couldn't wait to see Angela and Pride set off round the course.

She found Angela already up and sitting outside with a mug of tea, talking herself through the cross-country jumps.

'The water ditch,' she muttered. 'I've got to make sure I enter it at the right angle. And then there's that nasty triple bar near the beginning.'

'Good morning. Did you sleep okay?'

'Not really. I kept going through the course in my head, and now I've got terrible butterflies.'

'Be brave and go strong,' said Tilly. 'You know what Pride can do for you. You're both in great physical shape and you completely adore one another.'

'Thanks,' said Angela. 'But I can't help thinking about his leg. I know the vet says he's fine but his recovery just feels too good to be true and I'd never forgive myself if I made it worse by competing with him.'

Tilly smiled reassuringly. She could understand Angela's anxiety. She was sure she'd feel the same if it were her and Magic, but she had faith in the advice that Chief Four Paws and the vet had given.

When Tilly got down to the stables,
Pride was waiting at the door. He nickered
and pricked his ears. She felt happy that he
was pleased to see her. She'd spent time
with him before, but all the grooming and
cold water treatment had meant he'd grown
to trust her even more.

'So, here we are,' she said, rubbing
his neck. 'Cross-country day! Go well for
Angela, won't you?'

Pride lowered his eyelids. She tacked him up, checked and double checked everything, then led him to where Angela was waiting, ready to do some practice jumps before the competition began.

Pride seemed tense. It was as though he was sizing up the other horses. But when Angela emerged wearing her team colours, a white polo shirt with a red and blue stripe on the side, he immediately relaxed. He stepped towards her and gave a keen whinny.

Tilly realised it was best to give them some alone time together. She watched them working quietly from a distance.

When Angela and Pride's names were finally called, she mouthed 'good luck' and waved as they trotted up to the start box. The timer reached zero and they were off. Tilly knew Brook and Chief Four Paws would be somewhere on the course, cheering them on, hopefully near that troublesome water ditch. But she also knew Angela wouldn't have time to notice them.

She'd be putting everything she had into keeping a good, fast rhythm and clearing the jumps.

As groom, Tilly had to wait at the finishing line, but she hoped she'd hear about Pride's progress from the commentators. She spotted Anna, standing by the fence.

'Hi again,' she said.

'Hi. How's Pride doing with the cross-country?'

'He's just about to go,' said Tilly. 'He's pretty fearless. I think he'll do well. What about Bright Star?'

'He was one of the first horses on the course this morning. The ground was hard, but he did okay. A lot of the riders are saying the jumps are tougher than ever this year. There's one triple bar, in particular . . .'

Tilly smiled, but her stomach flipped. Suddenly, she heard Angela's name. She held her breath as she listened.

'And it's a rider from Great Britain up now . . . Angela Fisher . . . new to

Kentucky . . . great landing! She's just attacked that rolltop and now she's flying down the bank! Flying! Magnificent start and . . . oh . . . oh, no! She's lost her stirrup just before the triple bar . . . '

Tilly clasped her hand over her mouth.

'They're circling . . . her horse, Pride and Joy . . . but wait, it looks as if they're going back and trying it again. Yes!!

They're over. A mistake like that will lose time but won't incur penalties because she didn't present at the fence. But they've been bold enough to keep going. Let's see what else this plucky horse and rider can do . . . '

She sighed. Anna gave her a reassuring nod. They might be behind the clock, but at least Angela and Pride were safe. Hopefully without any more pressure they could enjoy the rest of the course.

When they finally galloped through the finishing gate, Tilly cheered. She could tell Angela was happy because she punched her arm in the air and gave Pride a congratulatory pat. She ran towards them.

'How was it?' she said, breathless with excitement.

'Fantastic!' said Angela. 'I know we messed up that triple, but I don't care. It was such a buzz!'

'The commentator described you as 'plucky'!'

'Plucky? I like the sound of that!'

Angela dismounted and handed the reins to Tilly. Pride gave a whinny, then nudged her shoulder.

'Well done, boy!' she said. 'You did it! I knew you would. Just the show jumping to go now. Now, let's get you all washed down and cool, and get you a drink.'

Nine

Tilly, Angela and Brook had to take
Pride for a final veterinary inspection
the next day, to make sure he was still in
sound health after the cross-country. All
the horses had to go through the same
inspection, but Angela was worried.

'I hope the stress of the cross-country
hasn't made that leg flare up again. I hate
the thought of him being in pain. And
we're enjoying this so much. It would be
a shame to miss out on the final day. If he

doesn't pass we won't be eligible for the show jumping.'

'It seemed fine when I checked this morning,' said Tilly. 'I gave it some cold water just to make sure.'

They had a nervous wait while the vet carried out the inspection, but luckily she gave Pride the all-clear. In fact, she said he was in better shape than many of the other horses. She commended them for taking such good care of his health.

'I guess I owe you guys a thank you,' said Angela. 'Without your care and attention, and all of those cold water hose-downs, I don't think we'd have come this far. Tilly, you've been the best groom ever!'

'Any time,' said Tilly. 'Right. Let's go and get ready. I need to plait Pride's mane and you need to get your jacket and gloves. There are fences to jump!'

The show jumping course was one of the most challenging Tilly had ever seen. There were a few easy jumps to begin with, but the rest were scarily high and there were several tricky combinations to contend with.

She watched from the side with the other grooms, as the first few competitors failed to deliver a clear round. One horse lost his nerve halfway round and refused a large oxer. Another knocked poles down on every other jump. By the time it was Angela and Pride's turn, Tilly's insides were in knots.

The crowd fell silent as the bell rang and the clock started. Tilly held her breath. Angela got Pride into a good canter before they began. She needed to keep her wits about her because the time was tight. Luckily, they cleared the first fence effortlessly and landed with poise and balance.

Tilly soon realised there was nothing to worry about. Pride was a graceful jumper with an incredible stride and Angela

seemed more confident than ever. Tilly remembered what Angela had said about trust. It was clear that she and Pride trusted one another completely.

It wasn't just Tilly who was impressed with the round. The grooms standing next to her were nodding with approval.

'Impressive,' one of them said.

'That's one horse and rider to keep an eye on,' said another.

'Yes, there are a few good British talents coming through. I've heard good things about a horse called Bright Star too.'

Tilly giggled. Bright Star was the horse Anna groomed. She couldn't wait to tell her what she'd heard.

Pride jumped faultlessly. The oxers, the triple bars, the difficult combinations, none of them was too big a challenge. Angela kept her hands low the whole time, with a nice contact down the reins. Pride knew exactly what to do.

They finished the course with just one time fault, to a rapturous round of applause

from the audience. Tilly jumped up and down and looked across the arena. She caught sight of Brook. He was standing next to Chief Four Paws and they were both cheering as loudly as they could.

Tilly felt a mixture of relief and delight. She was so pleased they'd done well in the show jumping, but she was especially glad that Pride had got through it all without any leg trouble. After all, she knew how close it had been to disaster.

Later, as Tilly and Brook walked Pride back to the stables, exhilarated by Angela's success, Tilly stopped and stared at her brother.

'Can you believe that less than a week ago we were saying goodbye to Pride at the airport, worrying whether he'd fly okay? So much has happened since then. We've met Chief Four Paws.

We've finally found out more about our
birth mum. We have a grandfather who
watches over free-roaming wild Mustangs.
We've hung out at Kentucky Horse Park,
which is the coolest place ever. And best
of all, Angela and Pride have completed a
major four star three day event!'

'And maybe next year they'll get a place in the top ten.'

'It would have been the top ten this year if it hadn't been for the time penalties on the cross country when she lost her stirrup.'

'And then maybe the year after that . . .'

'They'll win!'

They laughed, but secretly, they both hoped it might be a real possibility.

Ten

'Well, I guess that's it,' said Angela.

They loaded their cases into the passenger cab of the horsebox, which had been sent by the Horse Transportation Company. Polly rode with them.

'How did it go?' she said.

'We had a great time,' said Angela.

'Good for you.'

Then it was time to say goodbye to Chief Four Paws and Free Spirit, who'd been waiting in the yard.

Suddenly, Tilly was overwhelmed.

'It's been so amazing to finally meet you,' she said, her voice wavering as she smiled at the Chief.

'You too,' he said.

Then he threw out his arms and pulled her and Brook into a group hug.

'I admire you both,' he said. 'I am proud to welcome you as members of our tribe. You understand how to live in harmony with horses. You have the spirit of my people.'

'Thank you,' said Brook.

'Don't thank me,' said the Chief. 'Just use it wisely. It is a gift.'

Tilly nodded. She thought of all the times she'd made connections with horses – there was Magic Spirit, of course, but also Red Admiral, the racehorse; Goliath, the gentle draught horse; Moonshadow, the famous Derby winner; Samson, the stallion who'd gone on to triumph in the Puissance at Olympia; and Pickle, her friend Cynthia's naughty show pony. There'd been horses she'd helped recover from injury, horses she'd calmed, horses she'd trained, horses she'd rescued. Everyone told her she had a natural way with them and now she knew it was in her blood. She had the gift of the tribe and she would definitely, she decided, use it wisely.

95

She thought of Magic Spirit and how much she was looking forward to seeing him again. Then she turned to Free Spirit and found herself caught in his cool, blue-eyed gaze.

'Sorry to have to say goodbye,' she said. 'But I'll come and visit one day soon. I'd love to visit Chief Four Paws and Running River and the Mustang herds myself.'

Free Spirit pricked his ears and nudged her hands with his nose. She reached up to stroke his neck.

'And thanks for the tail-hairs,' she whispered.

When Tilly, Brook, and Angela arrived back in the UK late in the afternoon, they were met at the airport by Mr and Mrs Redbrow and Tilly's younger brother, Adam.

'Was it fun?'

'Did you have a good competition?'

'It was great,' said Brook.

'Did it all according to plan?' said Mrs Redbrow.

'Well, at first, Pride had problems with his leg,' said Angela. 'But thanks to Tilly's care and a bit of coaching from a Mustang, it all came together.'

The Redbrows had lots more questions about the trip. The chatter continued for the whole journey. Tilly was delighted to see her family and she was looking forward

to sitting down with her mum and telling her about everything Chief Four Paws had revealed, but for now, the number one thing on her mind was seeing Magic Spirit. As they drove through the familiar lanes of North Cosford, her dad turned to her.

'So, Tiger Lil', straight home? Or shall we stop at Silver Shoe Farm?'

Tilly smiled.

He knew her too well.

As the white buildings of Silver Shoe came into view, despite the long flight and the hard work of the past week, Tilly felt re-energised. With a spring in her step, she jumped out of the car. She didn't stop to see who was in the yard. She simply ran, as fast as she could, down to the long field.

And there he was, beautiful Magic, swishing flies with his tail and munching grass. When he saw Tilly, he galloped towards her.

'Hello, boy!' she cried, as he nuzzled her neck. 'I'm so glad to see you!'

Magic nickered.

'It was a fantastic trip,' she said. 'Not just because of the competition, but because we got to meet Chief Four Paws and find out about our birth mum and the photograph.

And we met Free Spirit. You would have liked him.'

She stared at the bracelets around her wrist.

'They fixed it for me, you know?' she said, holding up the bracelet her birth mum had given her, which matched Brook's.

'It was coming loose, but Chief Four Paws took some hairs from Free Spirit's tail and tied it back together. You can hardly tell. The hairs are a perfect match. It's as if they've come from the same horse.'

Tilly gasped. She wondered why she hadn't grasped it before. She remembered what the Chief had said, that the young Free Spirit was a living connection between the past and present. The horse in the photograph with her mother was the original Free Spirit. She pictured the image in her mind. She knew every little detail, because she'd spent so long gazing at it.

She stared at Magic. She loved the fact that she could tell him anything.

'Wow,' she breathed. 'The original hairs of my bracelet came from Free Spirit, and now it's been repaired with tail-hairs from his son!'

She didn't need to say any more. Magic flicked his mane and gave a contented snort.

The two of them stayed like this for a while, in the middle of the long field. The grass blew in the breeze and the sun began to set.

'Perfect,' she said, looking out across the horizon. 'I don't think I've ever

been happier. I've got you. I've got the Redbrows. I've got Silver Shoe. I've got Brook. And now I've got a whole new family, my tribe!'

She tickled Magic's nose and felt his warm breath on her fingers.

'Everything's perfect.'

Pippa's Top Tips

It takes a special horse to be successful at a top three day event.

In dressage, horses have to be responsive, supple and elegant. It's a real test of concentration, which is why in all the training, it's important to teach your horse to respond to your aids, despite distractions.

For cross-country, horses need to be brave, athletic, and very fit in order to cope with the demands of the terrain and fences.

For show jumping, horses must be able to jump a clear round, so you need to be careful, because you don't want to spoil a good dressage and cross-country round with poles falling in the show jumping phase.

Watching top grooms at a major competition is an excellent starting point for a young rider. It's a chance to see the most experienced riders, grooms and horses in action, and learn a few tricks.

In addition to normal grooming duties – like mucking out, feeding, cleaning tack, grooming and tacking up – at shows and competitions, a groom will also have to help load the equipment, plait the horse's mane, hold the horse in the ring, and check on the horse at night.

Before the cross-country, it's always important to walk the course thoroughly and know exactly where you are going, what fences you have got to jump and what line of approach you are going to take to fences.

Heat in a horse's limb could mean a sign of injury. Hose the affected area down with cold water as often as possible and, if in doubt, seek advice from a vet or someone more experienced.

Always make sure your horse or pony is well cooled off after the cross country. If he's very hot and sweaty you will need a good sponge, plenty of water and a sweat scraper and make sure you keep walking him as well until he stops blowing (gets his breath back).

The best and most successful partnerships between horse and rider are all about confidence and trust.

For more about Tilly and Silver Shoe Farm –
including pony tips, quizzes and everything
you ever wanted to know about horses –
visit www.tillysponytails.co.uk

Have you discovered the other books in the
Tilly's Pony Tails series?

Tilly Redbrow doesn't just love horses,
she lives, breathes and dreams them too!
Warm and engaging stories are packed with
Pippa Funnell's expert advice on everything
you ever wanted to know about horses.

Pippa Funnell: *Follow Your Dreams*

Pippa Funnell as you've never seen her before.

Get to know Pippa – her loves, her hates, her
friends, her family. Meet her beautiful horses,
and take a sneaky peek at life on her gorgeous
farm. Find out how she prepares for important
competitions, trains and cares for her horses, and
still has the time to write Tilly's Pony Tails.

And discover how, with hard work, passion
and determination, you too can follow
your dreams, just like Pippa.

978 1 4440 0266 9
£6.99